To all my little readers, I hope this book is your guiding light through any cloud of doubt.

— Nima

For my lovely seaside friends in Northumberland

— Cally

LITTLE TIGER
LONDON

LITTLE TIGER
An imprint of Little Tiger Press Limited
1 Coda Studios, 189 Munster Road, London SW6 6AW
www.littletiger.co.uk
Imported into the EEA by Penguin Random House Ireland,
Morrison Chambers, 32 Nassau Street, Dublin D02 YH68
www.littletigerpress.com
First published in Great Britain 2025
Text copyright © Nima Patel 2025
Illustrations copyright © Cally Johnson-Isaacs 2025
A CIP catalogue record for this book is available
from the British Library • All rights reserved
Printed in China • ISBN: 978-1-83891-647-3
CPB/1400/2965/0325
1 2 3 4 5 6 7 8 9 10

The Forest Stewardship Council® (FSC®) is a global, not-for-profit organisation dedicated to the promotion of responsible forest management worldwide. FSC® defines standards based on agreed principles for responsible forest stewardship that are supported by environmental, social, and economic stakeholders. To learn more, visit www.fsc.org

My Thoughts and Me

Nima Patel

Cally Johnson-Isaacs

We all have our own inner world.
What is it like inside your head?

I think in pictures.

I think in words.

Can your inner voice be friendly?

Don't forget your packed lunch!

Maybe your brain gives you some helpful reminders!

Does it sometimes suggest some really silly things?

I wonder if I can...

cover my little sister in paint...

say SPLATTABUNGAROOOO.

Maybe your inner voice doesn't always feel so encouraging . . .

Some thoughts can feel
confusing and scary ...

especially when they
all barge in at once!

So, how can you help yourself feel better?

You could take a break for a while and do something you enjoy.

But what happens when taking a break isn't enough?

Then it's time to challenge our thoughts!

How does this thought make me **feel**?

When a thought is upsetting us, we can take a deep breath and try to . . .

let it go!

If a thought feels very heavy, we might need someone to help us unpack it.

It can also help to come back to
how we feel in this moment, right now.
What can you . . .

Returning to the here and now helps us to feel safe.

to believe them.

So, take your time.
Be kind to yourself.

Be your own **best friend!**

Dear Grown-ups,

Have you ever found yourselves struggling with negative self-talk? With that sneaky little (or maybe even loud) voice in your head telling you, "You can't do that!" or "You don't belong here!" Well, did you know that sometimes children deal with their own version of this voice too?

Growing up is like a rollercoaster ride, and sometimes its twists and turns can make kids doubt themselves. Negative self-talk may show up when they bump into challenges, compare themselves to others or deal with new people and situations.

That doesn't mean that negative self-talk is an unavoidable reality. Children don't come into this world feeling that they aren't enough. It's something they learn, which means it's something they can unlearn too. So can we, even as adults!

In the pages of this book, we want to empower children with the tools they need to nurture their own minds. Because the truth is: they do belong. They are enough. They can take up space in the world. And the sky is the limit!

Nima x